MW00901266

First Edition, 2021

Witch Way Publishing

Tonya Brown
3436 Magazine St
#460
New Orleans, LA 70115

www.witchwaypublishing.com

Author: Tonya A. Brown
Illustrator: Pisey Keo
Editor: Tonya A. Brown

Printed in the United States of America

ISBN 978-1-087-90985-1

Tutty Learns About Witches

The Tutty Witch Series

Dedicated to Sutton

GAMES

Tutty was a little nervous today. Her mama needed to go to a very important meeting, one that Tutty was not allowed to join. While this made her sad, she was going to be visiting her Aunt Alice for the day. So maybe it wouldn't be so bad.

Tutty hadn't seen her Aunt Alice in almost a year. A lot was happening in their lives that made it really difficult to visit, but her mama said she would have a lot of fun. Excited for a day of adventure, Tutty put on her sweater, tied her shoes, and went with her mother to the car.

On their way to visit Aunt Alice, Tutty imagined what their day would be like. Would there be board games? Would they play outside? Would there be puppies and kittens? Would they watch a movie? Would they bake goodies? The possibilities seemed endless.

When they arrived, Aunt Alice was waiting outside for them. The first thing Tutty noticed when she walked up was Aunt Alice's colorful skirt - it had every color of the rainbow, and Tutty knew she wanted a skirt like that one day. While mama and auntie hugged and talked about adult things, Tutty looked around. There were gnomes on the lawn, a broom on the porch, plants and herbs in the ground, and a little gray dog happily running around Tutty.

Once mama left, Aunt Alice and Tutty walked inside of her small home. She immediately saw a table full of colorful rocks and ran over happily, looking them over.

"What are these, auntie?" Tutty asked.

"These? Oh! They are crystals. Little parts of the earth that I have found or have been gifted to me. Aren't they nice?"

Tutty nodded happily. It was hard to take her eyes off of them. Some were tall and thin, others short and round, some were shiny, and some even reminded her of rainbows.

"What are they for?"

"Oh, all kinds of things! Happiness, protection, health, but you know what? Sometimes it's ok to just think they're pretty."

Tutty agreed.

"Would you like a cup of tea?" Aunt Alice asked as she walked over to a room full of dried herbs hanging from various knobs and hooks. It reminded Tutty of something out of a fairytale book.

"Yes, please." Tutty followed her into the room, and she realized it was the kitchen. Aunt Alice poured some water into a kettle before placing it on the stovetop. Then, taking three containers, she kneeled down and asked Tutty which one she wanted.

Looking at the three jars, one had purple flowers, yellow flowers, and green leaves.

"One is Lavender. It tastes like a pretty flower. One is chamomile. It makes you feel warm and cozy. One is peppermint. It tastes like candy canes. Which one would you like?"

Tutty pointed to the purple flowers. "Lavender, please."

About 10 minutes later, Aunt Alice handed Tutty a warm cup of tea, and she happily took a few sips. She was right. It tasted exactly how she thought flowers smelled. While she sat in her Auntie's big blue chair, she noticed a book sitting on the table. Placing her cup down carefully, she climbed down and walked over before touching it gently.

"Auntie, what is this?"

Aunt Alice walked over and opened the book for Tutty. It looked old and had all sorts of writings that she could not read.

"This is my spellbook."

"A spellbook?" Tutty was in awe. "Are you a witch?"

Aunt Alice nodded, "Yes, I am."

Tutty only knew witches from the movies she watched. The movies made witches look scary and mean, but Aunt Alice was friendly and happy. Tutty felt a little confused.

"Aunt Alice, I thought witches were mean, but you're not mean."

Aunt Alice turned a page showing Tutty a picture of the moon.

"Well, a long, long time ago, some very afraid people took their fear out on those who could not protect themselves. They thought of all the worst things they could think of and said that these people did them and that they were witches. They were wrong, but sadly some people still believe it."

"Oh," Tutty thought this over. "So people were scared, and they said bad things about witches. Does that make you sad?"

"Oh no. I feel sad for the people they mistreated, but I am happy to be who I am. Some people may not understand, but that's ok. They just believe old ideas."

"Don't worry. If anyone says anything bad about witches, I'll tell them the truth." Aunt Alice smiled.

Tutty walked over to another broom Aunt Alice had leaned against a wall.

"Can you fly on brooms?" She secretly hoped it was true and that maybe one day she could fly past the moon and touch it.

"Only when I am deep asleep," Aunt Alice said as she took the broom from Tutty. She then began to move the broom from left to right towards the front door. "But I can move energy with my broom and create spaces that feel safe and clean."

"Oh! That's how I feel when my mama lights candles before movie nights."

"Well, candles are magic, did you know that?"

Tutty's eyes lit up, and she shook her head no.

"Only with the help of our parents can we light them, but candles can be used to send our wishes out into the world." Aunt Alice walked over to her bookshelf and grabbed a few candles sitting there. "You can even pick a color you feel matches your wish if you want to."

Tutty had never heard such a thing, but she loved it.

Tutty saw Aunt Alice pull out what looked like a deck of cards.

"Oh, I love cards! Mama and I play with them all the time. Are we going to build houses?"

Aunt Alice sat down in front of Tutty and laid the cards out. "These are a bit different. While you can build houses with them, they are meant for something more special."

Tutty looked over the cards that she saw before her. They looked a lot different than the playing cards her mama had. She reached over and picked one up. It had a picture of a star.

"These are divination cards. I lay some out and based off of the pictures, I can tell stories, get ideas, understand things better, or help a friend who needs guidance."

It was then Aunt Alice's dog Erebus ran across some of the cards, and they scattered.

Erebus

"Oh no! Why did he do that?"

"It's ok!" Aunt Alice said, reassuring Tutty. "Erebus does that sometimes when I'm not taking the cards too seriously. He is my familiar."

"Familiar? Is that like black cats? Why do you not have a black cat?"

"Well, some witches do have black cats, but I have my little dog. Witches don't only have cats as companions. Sometimes they have dogs, cats, mice, spirits, or other guides. I was just lucky enough to find my sweet Erebus."

"Does he do spells with you?" Asked Tutty as Aunt Alice put her cards back in their safe place.

"Not always. Sometimes he gets my attention when I need to notice something. Sometimes he adds energy to my spells, and sometimes he looks at me, then I know a message he's trying to send me."

"Are all pets fa...fa..."

"Familiars?" Tutty nodded.

"No, some pets are just friends. A familiar is a spirit that helps the witch, and sometimes they come to us as animals."

Witch?

Now that Tutty thought about it, she realized that her mama also had cards, candles, brooms, and a close pet. Maybe she was a witch too! However, she didn't have a spellbook or a rainbow skirt.

"Are all witches like you, Aunt Alice?"

"No," she said, shaking her head. "There are all types of witches in the world. Just as there are all different types of people. Some witches have a group of magic workers called a coven. Some witches are from a long line of magic. Then some witches learned from their families. Witches like me felt different and knew they were witches but couldn't find others. So they taught themselves."

"Do you wish you had others to help you?"

"Sometimes, but each witch's journey is magical and special. Each type of path offers something different. However, it's very important to remember that just because a witch's journey looks different, that doesn't mean it's any better or worse than another. I am like no witch, and no witch is like me - and that's the most magical thing in the world."

Tutty spent the rest of their day together exploring all the exciting things in and around Aunt Alice's home. They talked to the gnomes, gardened, and even picked a few flowers for mama. As the day was coming to an end, Aunt Alice gave Tutty a small bag with a yellow candle and a mini- broom.

"This is for you to have so that you remember that you are magic." Tutty happily took the present and smiled wide.

"Is it ok if I give you a hug?" Aunt Alice asked, and when Tutty nodded, the two embraced.

It was then they heard a car pulling into the driveway. The two walked outside just as mama was coming to the door. Aunt Alice gave her the flowers, and as they talked, Tutty got into the car.

Soon they were on their way home, and Tutty stared out the window, thinking of all she had learned that day.

"What are you thinking about, Tutty?" Asked mama.

Tutty sighed dreamily. "I can't wait to be a witch."

About the Author

Tonya A. Brown

TONYA A. BROWN is a current resident of New Orleans, Louisiana, where she is the editor in chief of Witch Way Magazine as well as writer and host of the podcast The Witch Daily Show. Tonya is a Lenormand reader, medium, and magical guide for other witches. While she currently has no children, she loves being an auntie.

Write to author Tonya A Brown
tuttytheseries@gmail.com

CPSIA information can be obtained
at www.ICGtesting.com
Printed in the USA
BVHW021723290721
613178BV00022B/1026